GREEN BEAR

ALAN ROGERS

Library of Congress Cataloging-in-Publication Data
Rogers, Alan, 1952-
        Green Bear / Alan Rogers.
            p. cm. -- (Little giants)
        "First published in the United Kingdom by
Two-Can Publishing Ltd."--T.p. verso.
        Summary: Green Bear changes the color of his
house to match the changing seasons.
        ISBN 0-8368-0406-6
        [1. Seasons--Fiction. 2. Color--Fiction. 3. Bears--
Fiction. 4. Dwellings--Fiction.] I. Title. II. Series:
Rogers, Alan, 1952- Little giants.
PZ7.R62555Gr 1990
[E]--dc20   90-9831

This North American edition first published in 1990 by
Gareth Stevens Children's Books
1555 North RiverCenter Drive, Suite 201
Milwaukee, Wisconsin 53212, USA

Printed in the United States of America

2 3 4 5 6 7 8 9 9 96 95 94 93 92 91

Green Bear likes green best.

He lives in the Green Forest.

Green Bear's house is green
outside . . .

and green inside.

But in autumn the Green Forest
turns orange . . .

so Green Bear paints his house
orange.

In winter the Green Forest is the color of snow . . .

so Green Bear paints his house white.

In spring the Green Forest turns
pink . . .

so Green Bear paints his house
pink.

While the pink paint dries . . .

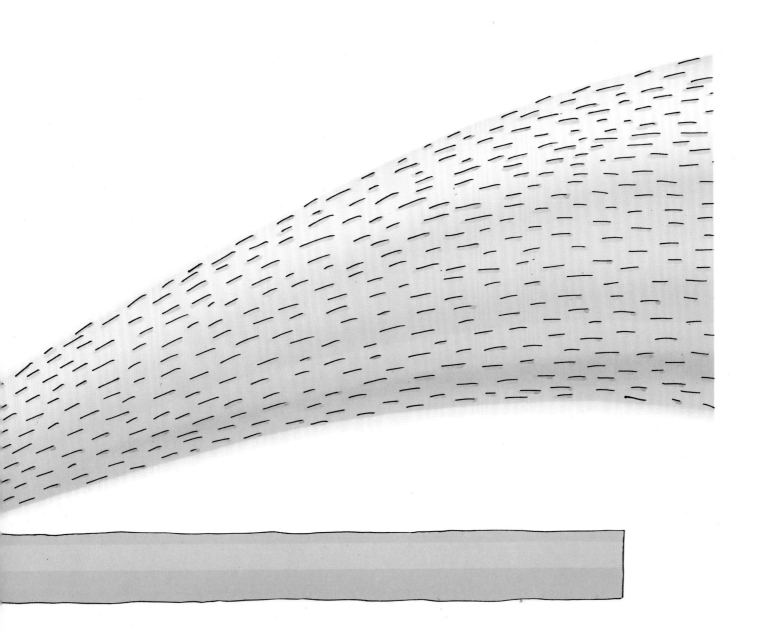

Green Bear mows the green grass.

The green grass sticks to the wet
paint . . .

but luckily, Green Bear likes green best.

SNIP!